POD RACER

LEVEL UP

POD RACER

R.T. MARTIN

darbycreek

MINNEAPOLIS

Darby Creek
A division of Lerner Publishing Group, Inc.
241 First Avenue North
Minneapolis, MN 55401 USA

For reading levels and more information, look up this title at www.lernerbooks.com.

Images in this book used with the permission of: © iStockphoto.com/gremlin (spaceship), © iStockphoto.com/Thoth_Adan (grunge background).

Main body text set in Janson Text LT Std 12/17.5.
Typeface provided by Adobe Systems.

Library of Congress Cataloging-in-Publication Data

The Cataloging-in-Publication Data for Pod Racer is on file at the Library of Congress.
ISBN 978-1-5124-3988-5 (lib. bdg.)
ISBN 978-1-5124-5358-4 (pbk.)
ISBN 978-1-5124-4877-1 (EB pdf)

LC record available at https://lccn.loc.gov/2016048281

Manufactured in the United States of America
1-42237-25786-3/16/2017

For my nephew, Will

It is the year 2089. Virtual reality games are part of everyday life, and one company—L33T CORP—is behind the most popular games. Though most people are familiar with L33T CORP, few know much about what happens behind the scenes of the megacorporation.

L33T CORP has developed a new virtual reality game: *Level Up*. It contains more than one thousand unique virtual realities for gamers to play. But the company needs testers to smooth out glitches. Teenagers from around the country are chosen for this task and, suddenly, they find themselves in the middle of a video game. The company gives them a warning—win the game, or be trapped within it. Forever.

CHAPTER 1

"Oh, you've got to be kidding me." That voice sounded familiar. A11_4_ON3 typed in his gamertag before he looked up to confirm who it was.

When the keyboard faded away, he saw ECHO standing there dressed in a red jumpsuit—the same as the one he was wearing. Behind her were two other players—STR33T_WIZE and Z1P_ZAP—dressed identically.

ECHO was glaring at him, standing with her hands on her hips. "'All For One' . . . really? When did you change your tag?"

"After I quit racing with you and started competing as a solo racer," he replied.

"You mean when *we told you* to stop racing with us," she spat back.

They were on the right side of the starting line. Behind ECHO and his other former teammates, he could see more racers milling about around pods of different glowing colors. He looked down at his jumpsuit—red. So was the pod he had been placed next to. All three of the others' jumpsuits and pods were red. This wasn't good—they'd been placed on the same team.

They had once been a racing crew, but that was over, and A11_4_ON3 had never intended to play another game with these three again. Just seeing them standing there made him flush with anger.

Their last race together had ended badly, and the other three had blamed him.

Well, he thought, *mostly ECHO and Z1P. STR33T was silent through the whole fight.* ECHO and Z1P_ZAP had called him selfish. He'd said he would be better off with racers at his own level. It ended with ECHO, always the team leader, asking him to leave their crew. Z1P_ZAP quickly agreed with her. He was sure STR33T_WIZE had made some halfhearted joke at the end of the fight, but he couldn't remember what it was.

It was fine. A11_4_ON3 wanted to do solo racing anyway. He hadn't had any intention of rejoining them. It was cruel fate that he was here now.

Z1P_ZAP crossed her arms. "Let's ask for a new teammate."

A new voice interrupted them. "Welcome to *Pod Racer!*" A man was standing in the middle of the track in a white suit with sunglasses covering his eyes. "You are the first sixteen people to play this remarkable L33T C0RP game. I am the Game Runner, and I'll be explaining how things work here."

"Excuse me!" Z1P_ZAP shouted. "We'd like a new teammate!" She pointed right at A11_4_ON3. "We don't want to play with this one."

The Game Runner tilted his head. "I'm sorry. Team selection has been locked. There will be no changes." It was final. They would be the red team. A11_4_ON3 looked at the others farther down the starting line: blue, then green, and yellow at the last starting position.

"As I was saying," the Game Runner continued, "you have been divided into four teams of four. This game is made up of three races. Before each race, you will compete in an arena to earn credits. With those credits, you can purchase upgrades to your pod, giving you an edge in the next race."

"What are you even doing here?" ECHO hissed to A11_4_ON3. "I thought you only did *solo* races now."

"I wouldn't miss a chance to try the new L33T game," he said. "I was assigned randomly to a team that needed one more. If I'd known it was you three, I wouldn't be here."

She scowled back at him.

"The losing team at the end of each race will be eliminated from the competition," the Game Runner continued to explain. "This—" he gestured to the track behind him—"is a qualifying race. It will not count for points, but it will allow you to get a feeling for your pods as well as assess the skills of your opponents."

"We'd like to quit!" ECHO shouted suddenly. A11_4_ON3, STR33T_WIZE, and Z1P_ZAP snapped their heads toward her.

"Excuse me?" the Game Runner asked.

"We'd like to quit," she said again, calmer this time.

The Game Runner smiled. "This is an extreme racing experience. You don't quit— you win. The losers in this competition will continue racing other teams until they are victorious. That's the only way you're getting out of here."

ECHO, Z1P_ZAP, and STR33T_WIZE all looked at A11_4_ON3. He looked down and shook his head. *This is not good*, he thought. *I'm going to wind up trapped in this game forever, racing with people I don't like and who don't like me.*

"It's time to get in your pods," the Game Runner instructed. "The qualifying race will begin shortly."

CHAPTER 2

The track for the qualifying race was just a straight path bordered by two bright red lines. It was wide enough for all sixteen pods to line up next to each other with little space to spare. Other than the lines, there was just darkness— the most basic of basic tracks.

The pods were smooth and sleek. They looked like cars except that every edge had been rounded off, leaving them without any corners. All of them were identical, each glowing in the color of its team. They hovered just slightly off the ground with two engines on the back. The tops of the pods opened up for the drivers to get inside.

"Just try to stay out of our way," ECHO said, climbing into her pod.

"I'm going to win the race. That's what I do," A11_4_ON3 snapped as he climbed into his own. "If you're in my way, I'm going to plow right through you." His pod closed around him. Through the clear glass top, he could still see ECHO glaring.

Inside there were several control features. The dashboard glowed with meters displaying the pod's speed as well as engine heat and distance traveled. A monitor off to the right served as a rearview mirror and there was a map screen next to it. The steering wheel looked exactly like one from a car, but there were no foot pedals. Instead, on the right-hand side was a lever that functioned as a throttle. The farther the driver pushed it forward, the faster the pod would go. Next to the throttle was a hand brake for quick turns. There was also a button labeled "weapon," but it wasn't illuminated like everything else inside.

"We're on the same team! *Don't* try to shove us out of the way," ECHO's voice sounded in his pod.

Great, thought A11_4_ON3. *There's a comm link.*

He looked around for some button or switch to turn off the radio communicator so he wouldn't have to listen to his so-called teammates, but he couldn't find one. "Don't get in my way," he said. "Then I won't have to get you out of my way."

"Wait!" STR33T_WIZE shouted through the comm. "I've got an idea. What if we all acted like friends for just a few races? Wouldn't that be crazy? Let's do it! Gooooo team!"

"No," ECHO said. "If he's going to treat us like any other racer, we do the same to him."

"Let me hear you say *Red! Team!*"

STR33T_WIZE ignored her. No one took part in his cheerleading chant. "Give me an *R*," he tried again, but once again no one responded.

A11_4_ON3 shook his head. *That guy hasn't changed at all.* He used to like STR33T_WIZE's unending positivity, but now it was just irritating.

The track boundaries turned yellow, signaling the race was about to begin.

A11_4_ON3 put his hand on the throttle, waiting for the lines to turn to green. He pictured himself crossing the finish line ahead of everyone else. He didn't care about ECHO, Z1P_ZAP, or STR33T_WIZE. They were the ones who told him to stop racing with them. Now was his opportunity to show them how much of a mistake that had been. He'd leave them all in his virtual dust.

"You guys ready?" ECHO asked.

A11_4_ON3 rolled his eyes. He knew what they were about to say. He'd said it himself more times than he could count. It was a ritual—a team motto they would say just before the start of each race.

"In it to win it!" ECHO, Z1P_ZAP, and STR33T_WIZE all said in unison, while A11_4_ON3 remained silent. The phrase used to get him excited to start a race, but now it was just annoying to hear.

The lines turned green. A11_4_ON3 slammed the throttle forward, and the pod took off. The vehicle was faster than he expected, but he adjusted quickly—just like he always did in a new racing game. The first part of the race was a straight line. Most of the players had fast reflexes and had managed to push the throttle down the moment the lines had turned green. So the majority of the pods were temporarily tied for first, with a few trailing slightly. A11_4_ON3 could see in his rearview monitor that one of the blue and two of the yellow racers had hesitated for just a moment before they'd accelerated.

The red team was perfectly in sync—all of them had managed to hit the throttle at the exact right moment. To his left, A11_4_ON3 could see ECHO through her pod's windshield. She kept her eyes locked on the track, ready for the first turn. He didn't bother to look at STR33T_WIZE on his other side. The only racer that might have a chance at beating him was ECHO. The other two were good, but they were also sloppy—not as precise as either ECHO or himself in their turns or use of the hand brake. She was the threat.

Here we go, thought A11_4_ON3 as the track ahead curved to the left. *Now they get to see what I'm made of.*

He eased up on his throttle, dropping back from the group one pod length and moving into position behind ECHO. If he could eliminate her from being a serious contender, he could easily walk away with this race.

Z1P_ZAP's voice came over the comm. "What's he doing?"

"Don't worry about him," ECHO said. "Focus on the race. Treat him like any other racer."

They reached the curve. A11_4_ON3 slid into place so that he was just to the left, behind ECHO. She did exactly what he thought she would do: followed the track's curve and stuck close to her team. She slowed slightly to keep control of her turn.

A11_4_ON3 didn't slow down. He slammed the throttle as hard as he could and continued going straight rather than following the turn. He smashed into the back left corner of ECHO's pod. The impact spun her so that she was facing the wrong way. She should have braked, but instead she tried to correct her position. Obviously she hadn't been expecting the hit.

"What are you doing?" she shouted at him.

"Winning," he replied, smiling as he saw her hit the broadside of STR33T_WIZE's pod on the rearview monitor. In his efforts to avoid the crash, STR33T_WIZE bumped Z1P_ZAP, pushing her into the edge of the track. She bounced back but at an angle that forced her to cross the track sideways. She lost a lot of ground to the other racers.

Hitting ECHO had worked better than A11_4_ON3 had expected. He thought she would have driven straight off the track. There was no visible wall keeping them in, just the red line on the ground, but her bounce had actually worked better. Not only had he bumped himself into perfect position to accelerate and get the inside track, but she had accidentally taken out her whole team—perfect.

The map screen displayed the positions of all the players in the race. ECHO was now dead last. STR33T_WIZE and Z1P_ZAP were barely ahead of her. A11_4_ON3 was in eighth place, but that wouldn't be a problem. Without having to deal with the others, he could easily maneuver his way into first. Besides, even if he didn't win, this was just a qualifying race. What was important was that he had made a statement to ECHO—he refused to work with her.

He relaxed in his seat as he listened to the other racers on his team scramble to regain a decent position in the race.

"If we focus, we can get ahead of some of those yellow racers," ECHO advised.

"That was a nasty trick," Z1P_ZAP muttered. "We could be winning right now."

A11_4_ON3 didn't bother responding, focusing entirely on the race now. He swerved and accelerated his way into fifth place, then fourth, third, second, and, after some back and forth with a green racer, managed to pull into first place. Now all he had to do was maintain his position.

The track was basic, but not altogether easy. Some of the turns were quite sharp, requiring use of the hand brake to make the inside of the curve. About halfway through, the course formed a spiral, forcing the racers to make a right turn for nearly a full minute.

Once he made it past the spiral, A11_4_ON3 checked on the other racers' positions. He had a comfortable lead. His teammates were still lagging behind in the bottom three positions. He smiled to himself again. *That'll show them.*

After a few more turns and curves, he saw the finish line. He pushed the throttle all the way down, bringing his pod to max speed for the big finish. When he crossed the line, the pod slowed to a stop. The rest of his team had not improved their position despite their best efforts, coming in fourteenth, fifteenth, and sixteenth place. They'd made up some of the ground they had lost after the crash, but not enough to get a respectable finishing position.

As ECHO crossed the finish line in last place, the teams' standings appeared on the dashboards of the pods. A11_4_ON3 frowned at the standings, though they didn't exactly surprise him.

The red team was in last place.

Even though he'd come in first, the other three coming in last meant their team's overall score was significantly worse than any of the other teams'.

"I hope you're happy," ECHO snapped over the radio. Their four pods had been brought together when the race ended, and now they could all glare at each other through their windshields. "See what happens when you don't work with the rest of your team?"

"I told you to stay out of my way!" he shouted back at her.

"We weren't in your way," Z1P_ZAP chimed in. "You could have left us alone."

A11_4_ON3 rolled his eyes. "It's just a qualifying race. It doesn't matter."

"Well," ECHO said, "now we know where you stand." She paused for a moment, then looked to the other two. "We'll have to win this in spite of him."

"Gooooo team," STR33T_WIZE said sadly.

LEVEL 1

CHAPTER 3

A11_4_ON3 sat in his pod, refusing to make eye contact with the other red racers as he waited for the next level to load.

"You know we lost thanks to you, right?" ECHO snapped.

"*I* won," A11_4_ON3 replied. "It's not my fault you couldn't recover from a crash."

"It was your fault we crashed in the first place!" shouted Z1P_ZAP.

"I'm just going to pitch this idea again," STR33T_WIZE said. "What if we worked as an actual team and didn't try to make one another lose? Do you guys think that would be a good strategy?"

"It's hard to work as a team when one of your members is a selfish jerk," Z1P_ZAP muttered.

The qualifying race statistics faded away from the dashboard, and the arena for the battle came into view—fuzzy at first, but it got clearer as it finished loading. The arena was huge—three levels tall, connected by ramps. The walls were green lasers. The new map on-screen showed the positions of all the racers: each of the teams started on their own side of the square battlefield on the lowest level, all pointed toward the center.

Inside A11_4_ON3's pod, the red weapon button lit up near the controls. Looking at the other pods, he could see they each had large, mounted laser cannons on the tops of their pods.

"Welcome to the arena!" It was the Game Runner. They couldn't see him this time, but A11_4_ON3 recognized the voice. "Here, you will battle in a game of laser tag to the last team standing. Your success or failure here will not affect your standing in the next race, but you will earn credits for each hit you make. Each of you has a laser cannon mounted to the top of your pod. The trigger on the far right of your control panel fires the cannon. You will get one thousand credits for each racer you eliminate. Each time you fire your laser, it takes thirty seconds to recharge. It only takes one shot to disable a pod, but be careful: friendly fire is activated. That means if you shoot one of your teammates, they will be eliminated, and you will not receive credits for the hit."

"So there's no advantage to shooting us," ECHO said, clearly directing the comment toward A11_4_ON3.

"At the end of the battle," the Game Runner continued, "you may use your credits to purchase upgrades for your pods to be used in later races and battles." He paused for a moment, then said, "Let the battle begin!"

ECHO, Z1P_ZAP, and STR33T_WIZE all took off as fast as they could, diving into the arena. A11_4_ON3 waited, holding back to let the other racers enter the arena first. He'd wait until he could see one of them, then chase them down—better to find a racer to tail than dive into the arena blindly.

"Okay, let's stick together," he heard ECHO say to the others. "And watch your shots. We don't want to eliminate one another."

"It's not our shots we need to watch," Z1P_ZAP said. A11_4_ON3 smirked to himself, but he wouldn't take them out. There wasn't any benefit if he wouldn't get credits for it.

Except maybe to prove a point again, he mused.

"Three green pods just went up to the second level," STR33T_WIZE said.

It took longer than he thought it would before another racer finally came into view again. A11_4_ON3 had been waiting for nearly two full minutes before he saw a blue pod speed by the entrance to the arena directly in front of him.

He sped inside and made a sharp right just in time to see the blue racer make a left behind a wall. The inside of the arena was a maze. Random walls and ramps to the other levels had been placed around to allow players to dodge and maneuver out of the line of fire. He followed the blue racer, checking his rearview to make sure someone wasn't stalking him too. They continued through three rooms, but when the pod turned to head up a ramp, A11_4_ON3 was in perfect position. He fired, and the blue pod glowed bright for an instant then vanished. A cooldown timer started on his dashboard—thirty seconds until he could fire again, but he had just earned one thousand credits.

His teammates were chattering about taking down the green pods they'd followed up the ramp. It sounded like they were having some trouble, unable to get into position to fire. He was actually surprised when Z1P_ZAP excitedly shouted, "Got 'em!"

Just as his countdown reached zero and his cannon was ready to fire again, a yellow racer pulled right in front of him from around a corner. A11_4_ON3 didn't waste any time. He immediately fired again, taking out the racer and restarting his countdown timer.

On the map, he could see racers starting to drop like flies, but his team seemed to be doing reasonably well. The yellow team only had one racer left after the one he had taken out. The green and blue teams both had three racers left.

"No, no, no!" STR33T_WIZE yelled. "They got me." One red dot on the map disappeared.

"Ha!" ECHO shouted. "I got him back for you at least." A green dot disappeared.

A11_4_ON3 chased the last yellow player up onto the third level of the arena, around a corner, and down a narrow passage. The yellow player was heading for an opening in the wall—a bottleneck. A11_4_ON3 pointed his pod right at the opening, but this would take perfect timing. Just as the yellow racer went through the doorway, he pulled the trigger—a direct hit! The racer disappeared.

There were still two blue racers and one green left. He drove back down to the second level and caught sight of one of the blue racers. The pod was going relatively slow. *This should be an easy shot once I close in*, he thought to himself. In his rearview, he saw ECHO and Z1P_ZAP swoop in behind him.

"This guy's mine," he said. "Back off."

"This is for the qualifying race," Z1P_ZAP said.

"No!" shouted ECHO, but it was too late. A11_4_ON3's controls went dead. The steering wheel locked into place. His pod started vibrating, and all of the dials turned bright red. She'd shot him—she'd actually shot him.

"*Are you kidding me?!*" he shouted over the group's radio. "What was that for?"

"I told you—the qualifying race," Z1P_ZAP replied.

"You shouldn't have done that," ECHO said. "It wasn't worth it."

His display faded out and an overhead view of the arena replaced it. He could see through the walls—able to view the entire battle, but only as an observer. He watched as ECHO easily took down the blue racer he had been stalking.

"I just want to go on record saying I wasn't involved in that," STR33T_WIZE said, but

A11_4_ON3 couldn't see him, even though they'd both been eliminated.

Z1P_ZAP said, "What did we learn, children?"

CHAPTER 4

Neither Z1P_ZAP nor ECHO was the last pod standing. While their lasers cooled down, the last green player took out Z1P_ZAP. Just as her cooldown time finished, ECHO was able to pull a one-eighty and take out that racer, but the last blue player shot her while she was vulnerable.

The arena faded away and a menu appeared in front of A11_4_ON3. It was a list of upgrades he could make to his pod. Some of them enhanced the performance of the vehicle. Others were weapons the driver could use to disable other racers.

"Two of us should buy speed upgrades,"

ECHO said. "The other one should get a weapon or two for defense."

Though he couldn't see them because of the menu screen blocking his view, A11_4_ON3 could tell he wasn't included in their plan. That was no problem. He didn't intend to work with them anyway. Z1P_ZAP had lost him a thousand credits and maybe a victory in the arena by shooting him.

"I'll get the weapon," STR33T_WIZE said. "This laser looks awesome!"

"What's it do?" Z1P_ZAP asked.

"Stops a racer cold for ten seconds."

"Great," ECHO said. "Z1P and I will get the speed upgrades. I'm also going to upgrade my handling, since I have the extra credits."

A11_4_ON3 tried to ignore them, looking at the list of possibilities. He had three thousand credits to spend, and he intended to use every last one of them. He definitely wanted a speed upgrade. It cost fifteen hundred. He purchased it. He looked at the handling upgrade, also fifteen hundred. It would help to be able to make sharper turns without using the hand brake, but he dismissed it. The speed upgrade would be enough to give him an edge.

I need a weapon, he thought. *Just in case.* The laser that STR33T_WIZE bought cost two thousand credits. He couldn't afford that. He looked through the list for something cheaper and found one that he liked. It was called a "pusher." When he pulled the trigger, any racer that was too close to him would be pushed away. Like the cannon in the arena, it had a thirty-second cooldown timer. It cost exactly fifteen hundred—the rest of his credits—so he bought it.

When he was done, he was forced to wait while the rest of the racers finalized their purchases. He listened through the communicator as his teammates continued to strategize.

"Stay as close as you can, STR33T," ECHO instructed. "If you see someone moving up on us, blast 'em with the laser."

"I'll try to keep up," he said. "But you'll both be going a lot faster than I will. Remember, I don't have the speed upgrade."

"Do your best," she said. "Z1P, stay near me. We'll protect each other as much as we can."

"You got it," Z1P_ZAP said.

There was a long pause. Finally, ECHO asked, "Any chance you want in on this plan, CRU1S—"

"Don't call me that!" A11_4_ON3 snapped back at her. He'd abandoned the name CRU1S3R when they kicked him out of their crew. "That's not my name anymore."

"Whatever," ECHO said. "Do you want in on this or not? We'll do better as a team. Even you have to admit that."

He tried to think of something clever to say. "Nope," he responded instead. "You do whatever you want. I'm winning this race. Alone."

"Seriously? You *know* we need to win as a team," Z1P_ZAP said. "STR33T, make sure 'All For One' here is the first person you blast with that laser."

"No!" ECHO said. "We have to at least act like a team, and he's a good racer. If he gets in front of us, just let him go. Letting him win would be good for the whole team."

"Fake teamwork?" STR33T_WIZE asked. "I can live with that."

"I think he still needs to be put in his place," Z1P_ZAP continued. "Maybe coming in last will get the message through his thick skull."

"No," ECHO repeated. "We work as much like a team as we can. That means leaving him alone."

The race loaded. The pods were all lined up at the base of a volcano that was thousands of feet tall with molten lava spewing from the top. The red team was placed on the far left of the track. A dirt road ahead of them led straight into the volcano. This was going to be very different than the qualifying race.

The Game Runner once again appeared in front of them. "Welcome to the first race! You'll be driving into that," he said, smiling and pointing to the exploding mountain behind him. "You'll find the inside has been mostly hollowed out and the finish line is at the top. But be careful—the bottom is still a pool of boiling lava. If you fall in, you lose and will be placed in the lowest available finishing position. Remember, the team that finishes last in this race will be eliminated from the competition."

The Game Runner vanished and a countdown started down from ten on the pod's dashboard.

"Remember the plan," ECHO said over the comm link. "If we're going to have to race with A11_4_ON3, let's not get eliminated and have to start over again in another competition. Let's win this. Ready?"

"In it to win it!" they all said again.

A11_4_ON3 ignored them, instead visualizing himself coming in first place again. He pushed himself deeper into his seat and gripped the handle of the throttle harder, antsy to start. The countdown continued in front of the racers:

THREE
TWO
ONE
GO!

The racers took off. Once again, A11_4_ON3's pod sped off at the first possible moment. The speed upgrade was powerful— taking off at breakneck speed pushed him farther into his seat. Out of the corner of his eye, he saw ECHO was keeping perfect pace with him. Several of the racers on other teams must have also purchased the speed upgrade. The ones that hadn't were already beginning to fall behind.

They entered the volcano. The rocky path wound back and forth through the volcano's center. The track narrowed, only wide enough for two or sometimes three pods across. As the racers entered, some had to slow down and fall in line behind others to avoid hitting another pod or flying off the track. Three blue racers shot past the red team and took the three top positions. A11_4_ON3, ECHO, and Z1P_ZAP took the next three. STR33T_WIZE had fallen back into ninth place without the speed upgrade. Two yellow team members were between them.

The boiling lava below made the interior glow red and orange. Fireballs and falling rocks threatened to destroy the track or land in the racers' paths. There was a grumbling, constant roar only broken by louder explosions that actually shook the pods.

Keep your eyes on what's in front of you, A11_4_ON3 reminded himself. Immediately, the track curved right. ECHO got the inside of the turn and pulled slightly ahead of him, but he regained his position when the track curved left next. He also managed to pull ahead of one of the blue racers, but a green pod sped past him. *Enjoy it while you can*, he thought.

"STR33T," ECHO called out, "get this yellow guy off my tail."

"Way ahead of you," he replied. "Got him!"

In his rearview display, A11_4_ON3 saw a yellow racer stop in the middle of the track. Several other racers had to swerve to avoid hitting the halted pod.

Not bad, he thought, but he refused to give his so-called teammates any encouragement out loud.

The track was a constant incline. It twisted and turned all over the place, sometimes cutting across the middle of the volcano, but in other places hugging the outer wall, going higher and higher up toward the top. While the rumbling never stopped, sometimes the shaking shook the display on A11_4_ON3's pod and nearly caused him to lose control. Each time the rumbling got particularly bad, he could see other racers swerve all over the road as well.

All the pods were trying to stay close to the middle of the track. The road had no guard rail, so if a pod got too close to the edge, it could tip off the track and into the lava below.

A few minutes into the race, A11_4_ON3 had managed to pass two of the three blue racers in front of them. He could see ECHO in his rearview tailing only a little behind him. She had also managed to pass the blue racers, but just as he glanced at her, a yellow pod dodged to her right and pulled ahead, right behind A11_4_ON3.

The yellow pod moved up on him. A11_4_ON3 tried to nudge the racer off the track by steering left, but the yellow pod slowed down just before he collided with it. Instead of hitting the pod, he swerved to the left, nearly falling off the edge himself.

He gritted his teeth. When he thought he was about halfway up the volcano, he glanced at his rearview display. ECHO wasn't far behind him. The yellow racer that he had tried to nudge off the track had steadied and was positioned between them.

"You guys keeping up?" It was ECHO checking in with the rest of the team.

"Right behind you," Z1P_ZAP said.

"I'm falling behind," STR33T_WIZE said. "I need to get that speed upgrade next time. There's no way I can compete without it."

"You don't need to take first," ECHO reassured him. "We just need our combined score to be better than one other team's. I think we're doing fine. I'm in fourth and CRU—A11_4_ON3 is in second."

As they neared the top of the volcano, the turns got tighter and came more frequently. Occasionally, the turns were so sharp the drivers had to practically make a U-turn to stay on course. The bottom of the track seemed like a cakewalk compared to this, and *that* hadn't been easy.

A11_4_ON3 kept trying to get close enough to the blue racer in front of him to edge the player out or even just use the pusher weapon to throw the pod off, but this racer was good. When he tried to pass on the left, the driver moved into position to block his path. A11_4_ON3 shifted to pass on the right, but again, the driver blocked the attempt.

"Gah!" Z1P_ZAP shouted. "Someone hit me with the same laser STR33T's got. I can't move!"

"Okay," ECHO began, "don't panic. When you can move again, just—"

"Z1P, look out!" STR33T_WIZE shouted suddenly. "*Ahhhh*, I hit her! No, no, no! We're both off the track!"

"*What?*" Echo burst out. "What happened?"

There was silence over the comm. A11_4_ON3 was surprised to realize he felt bad for them. He shook off the feeling. *All I can do is take first*, he thought.

"I hit her while she was stopped."
STR33T_WIZE was breathing deeply. "I pushed her off the track, and I lost control and fell off myself. We both got eliminated. Sorry, Z1P."

"It's not your fault," she replied. "But we were the first two to fall off the track. We're in fifteenth and sixteenth place."

Out of sixteen racers, A11_4_ON3 thought. *The team's in dead last.*

CHAPTER 5

"We can't afford to come in anything but first and second," ECHO said, and A11_4_ON3 knew she was addressing him specifically. "We both have to get in front of that blue pod."

Great, he thought, *I'm not part of your plan, but I still have to clean up your mistakes.* Nevertheless, he pushed on the throttle and said, "I'll get in front of him."

He pushed his pod to the maximum speed though he noticed immediately that he was taking turns way too fast. He was coming close to the edge on a lot of them, but the extra speed was working—he was gaining on the blue racer.

They were almost at the top of the volcano. A11_4_ON3 was right on the blue pod's tail, but the track had narrowed—it was barely wide enough for two pods to drive next to each other—and the racer kept blocking any chance to pass.

A11_4_ON3 realized that passing the blue racer may not be the best option. He could easily get bumped off the track himself if the driver decided to bump him from behind. Instead of trying to pass, he got as close as he could, nearly touching the other pod. Just as the track made a sharp right, he fired the pusher. It worked exactly as he had hoped. The blue racer jolted forward from the push and didn't correct the pod's position in time. Instead of making the right turn, the pod flew off the track, down into the lava at the bottom.

"Nice move!" ECHO said, but A11_4_ON3 just smirked to himself.

It wasn't long until he saw the end. The track curved into a spiral that led to the top of the volcano. There he saw a glowing white line. He pushed his pod to maximum speed once again and flew across the line. ECHO finished right behind him. Their pods halted, and a list of the finishing positions appeared on the dashboard.

He and ECHO came in first and second place. The green team won overall, though, and the blue team came in second. The yellow team came in last, so they were eliminated— the red team was safe.

LEVEL 2

CHAPTER 6

"That was too close, guys," ECHO said as the arena loaded for the second round of laser tag. "We need to be more careful. Stupid mistakes like that are what will get us eliminated." She paused for a moment. "Thanks for your help back there, A11_4_ON3."

"Yeah, thanks buddy," STR33T_WIZE said. "You pulled some sweet moves in that race."

"I'm not thanking him," Z1P_ZAP snapped. "He's working against us—just trying to win for himself."

"Well in this case, that strategy worked," ECHO said. "If it hadn't been for him, a blue player would have taken first, and we would have lost to the yellow team. We kind of owe him one."

"Not going to happen," Z1P_ZAP insisted. He could picture her crossing her arms and glaring like she always did when something wasn't going her way.

"Thank you *so much*, A11_4_ON3," STR33T_WIZE said, imitating Z1P_ZAP's voice. "We should all work as a team, and you really helped us out back there. Teamwork— yay!" ECHO laughed, and even A11_4_ON3 couldn't help from chuckling a little.

"Shut up, STR33T," Z1P_ZAP muttered. "And I *don't* sound like that!"

When the laser tag arena appeared again, it was only two levels high this time. Once again, each team started on their own side of the square, but this time one of the sides was unoccupied.

"Okay," ECHO said as the countdown started, "let's watch each other's backs."

"I'm still not trusting A11_4_ON3," Z1P_ZAP replied.

He rolled his eyes. "You're the one who shot *me*, remember?"

"That won't happen again," ECHO said. "We need you if we're going to win this thing. Z1P, you absolutely must not eliminate A11_4_ON3, got it?"

"I can't promise anything," she said. He could practically hear her sneering from inside her pod.

"You do what you like," he said. "I'll win on my own. I've said it before, and I'll say it again—stay out of my way."

The countdown reached zero, and his teammates sped off into the arena, but A11_4_ON3 was going to use the same strategy he used last time. It didn't take as long this time. A green pod moved slowly by the entrance right in front of him. He sped into the arena to chase after it—an easy target.

The moment he entered, he realized he had made a huge mistake. As he closed in on the pod, he saw three other green pods waiting for him to enter. He dodged the first laser, but moments after that, his pod began to vibrate and his controls glowed bright red. He'd been hit.

He slapped his palm to his forehead. The green team knew his strategy. The pod he'd seen was bait, and he'd gone for it like an idiot.

"Green got me," he informed his team, feeling his cheeks get hot. "They waited for me to enter the arena. They knew I was coming."

"I'll get them back," STR33T_WIZE said.

"No," ECHO said, "don't leave the group!"

"I got this!" he shouted back. There was a pause in the conversation, but it was broken by STR33T_WIZE shouting, "They're all down here—all four of the green team! I missed the shot! They're after me!" He didn't stand a chance. He was eliminated next.

ECHO and Z1P_ZAP were up on the second level of the arena when the blue team arrived in force. Slowly but methodically, the four blue team members backed the remaining red teammates into a corner. ECHO was able to hit one of them by swooping around a wall when the player wasn't paying enough attention, but she was quickly eliminated while her laser charged up again. She was the only one who was able to score any points. Z1P_ ZAP took a shot but missed and got eliminated.

They had to watch the green team and three blue players battle it out. In the end the green team won, with two players remaining. The teams had used similar tactics in their gameplay: multiple players worked together to isolate a single pod, drawing it away from its group and then pushing it into a corner. It was obvious why the red team had lost so spectacularly—the other teams were working together. Most of the red team had been isolated to begin with. First A11_4_ON3 had peeled away, and then STR33T_WIZE had driven off alone. ECHO and Z1P_ZAP never stood a chance once they were gone.

When the upgrade purchase screen loaded, A11_4_ON3 had to say he was finished without purchasing anything. Only ECHO would be able to purchase an upgrade, and probably not a very powerful one. In the next race, the green and the blue teams would have a massive advantage.

CHAPTER 7

"What did you buy, ECHO?" Z1P_ZAP asked.

"A magnet," she replied.

"A magnet?"

"Yeah," she said, "I figure I might be able to stop one of you from falling off a track by drawing you closer to my pod. It only works for five seconds with a thirty-second cooldown time, though, so we can't use it unless we need to."

Not a bad idea, A11_4_ON3 thought, but again, he wouldn't say it out loud.

While he waited, he thought about what racing had been like when he was in their crew. They'd been good—really good. They'd won almost every race they entered. In races with weapons, they would watch each other's backs, taking out anyone that was trying to nudge them out of the way. In races without weapons, they'd still move as a squad, blocking other racers' attempts to pass by. They raced in cars, boats, planes . . . one race had even had them in giant hamster balls rolling toward the finish line.

A11_4_ON3 couldn't quite remember when things started to go wrong. Maybe he'd gotten sick of taking second or third place so that someone else on his team could take first. He remembered thinking about solo racing a lot near the time of his departure. It seemed easier, simpler. All he had to do was take first. He didn't have to worry about keeping track of teammates or cleaning up their mistakes, making sure they were safe.

He'd done well as a solo racer too, maybe not as well as they'd done as a team, but well enough. There was one aspect of solo racing that he loved above all else—when he won, his victories were his own. He didn't have to share the position of first place with anyone else. His victories were his doing, and no one could take that away from him.

The next race loaded, and immediately he felt his heart sink when he saw the track. Not only was he going into this race without any upgrades, but the conditions of this race were far different than the volcano.

The pods were lined up on an ice sheet, but that was about all he could see of the track. There was a blizzard raging over this race. He could feel the wind pushing the pod, threatening to flip it over. At high speeds, it could present a serious problem. During the last race, he'd noticed how realistic the physics of this game were. All it would take was a strong gust to lift a pod off the track, send it airborne, and cause a disaster for the driver.

"Gamers," A11_4_ON3 heard the Game Runner say, "welcome to the second race! Only three teams remain, and one more will be eliminated at the end of this track." He couldn't see where the voice was coming from because the snow ruined any visibility. "As you can see, this race takes place on a glacier. Once again, if you fall off the track, you will be placed in the lowest possible finishing position. Unlike the volcano, this track is slipperier than you'll be used to. And be careful of the wind gusts—they can whip your pod around faster than you might think. Everyone ready?" He didn't wait for an answer. "Let's get started!" The countdown from ten started.

"Okay," ECHO said as the racers revved their engines, "everyone stay close to me. If you start sliding close to the edge of the track, I'll engage the magnet and keep you close. You should follow behind me the whole time."

A11_4_ON3 looked at ECHO's pod. There was a large, silver cylinder, which he figured was the magnet, fixed to the top of it now.

"I'll be on your left," Z1P_ZAP said.

"I'll take the right," STR33T_WIZE added.

"Sounds good," ECHO confirmed. "Z1P, we're going to have to go a little slower. STR33T doesn't have the speed upgrade yet, and we definitely need to stick together through this." She paused for a moment. "You're welcome to stick with me too, A11_4_ON3. You'd have to stay behind me though. I need to be able to see where I'm going."

A11_4_ON3 didn't like the sound of that. Not only did it mean that he couldn't take first, but it also meant that he wouldn't be able to see where he was going. He'd have to trust ECHO to take the whole team to the finish line by herself.

THREE
TWO
ONE
GO!

"I'll pass," he said, slamming down on the throttle.

This time he was prepared for the force of the pod accelerating so quickly, but the Game Runner hadn't been kidding. The wind was stronger than A11_4_ON3 had anticipated. As soon as he was in motion, he found he actually had fairly little control over his pod. The wind pushed it to the right, so he steered left to compensate, but when the wind suddenly died down, his pod made a sharp left. When he compensated for that, the wind picked up again and pushed him to the right. The snow was so heavy that he could barely see what was around him. It was all a blur of white. Each time he swerved, he worried he would fly off the edge of the glacier.

Even when the wind wasn't affecting his driving, his turns weren't as sharp as they had been in the volcano. Rather than turning, he was really only able to slide around on the glacier.

In his rearview display, the few other racers he could see were having as difficult of a time as he was. Pods were slipping and sliding all over the track. He caught quick flashes of red—his three teammates, trailing a bit behind him, and they were having trouble staying together. He saw ECHO's pod pinballing off of Z1P_ZAP and STR33T_WIZE. Each time she hit them, they bounced farther and farther away from each other.

"You need to straighten out your path," ECHO said.

"What do you think we're trying to do?" STR33T_WIZE responded.

"It's impossible to just go straight," Z1P_ZAP chimed in. "I keep turning or drifting."

"Stay as close to me as you can," ECHO reminded her teammates. "If you need me to engage the magnet to keep you close, just say so."

A11_4_ON3 had to admit that he wasn't faring much better than his team. He hadn't even reached top speed yet. The drifting forced him to keep lowering the throttle to get control of the pod. Every time he tried to speed up, the wind pushed him around the track as if he were a flimsy leaf.

It was hard to tell who was in first place. He knew that at least one green team member was out in front of him, but he'd only seen one blue pod in his rearview—no way to know where the other three were.

There was one advantage to this course— there weren't any obstacles in the middle of the track. A11_4_ON3 hadn't expected any in the first race—always the easiest in video games—but he had suspected that the second race would have some sort of obstacle: rocks or jumps, something to increase the level of difficulty. As far as he could tell, this course was just a straight line, nothing in the way.

It took a while, but eventually he was able to figure out how to drive through the blizzard. All he had to do was hold back from pushing the throttle to top speed—it was just too fast for these conditions. Now that speed upgrade almost seemed like a waste of credits. He found he was able to anticipate the severity of the wind by watching the snowfall. If it was coming straight down, the wind didn't affect his pod, but if the snow started flying sideways, pushing him, he had to steer into the wind to compensate.

Other racers popped in and out of his view. He'd see them to the right or left, sometimes behind him. They'd swerve and turn, trying to make up for the push of the wind, but they all eventually faded away, disappearing back into the snow.

"I think I'm getting the hang of this," STR33T_WIZE said.

"Me too," Z1P_ZAP added.

"Good," ECHO replied. "We don't know what else will happen before the end, so still stay close."

A11_4_ON3 assumed that his teammates were behind him, although he couldn't see them through the blizzard. He focused on his own driving, wanting to take the highest possible finishing position. While that may not have technically counted as working with his team, his taking first would still benefit them. Each time the wind picked up, he lowered his throttle to regain control of his pod. When the wind died down, he pushed his pod as fast as he could for as long as he could.

Suddenly, A11_4_ON3 felt a new sensation in his pod: rumbling, just like he'd felt in the volcano. At first he wasn't sure if it was the wind picking up again or if this was some new challenge, but that question was answered when he saw cracks shoot down the middle of the track ahead of him.

"Oh, great," STR33T_WIZE said. "What's going on now? As if this wasn't hard enough to begin with!"

A11_4_ON3 knew exactly what was happening. "The glacier is breaking apart."

CHAPTER 8

More cracks appeared on the track. The
rumbling got stronger, and the wind seemed
to be getting worse. A11_4_ON3 tried to steer
his pod away from the cracks, but there were
so many of them that it was almost impossible.
He knew what they would do next—spread
and shift apart, creating giant gaping holes in
the track.

"Stay away from the cracks," ECHO told
her team.

"I'm having a hard enough time just staying
on the track," STR33T_WIZE replied.

A11_4_ON3 caught sight of his teammates
again. They were still behind him, but they'd

managed to fall into a line. All three were swerving to avoid the increasing number of cracks that appeared in the ice.

The cracks started to widen. The rumbling turned into a violent shaking. A11_4_ON3 saw a massive gap open up in the track right in front of him. He tried to steer to the left of it, but the wind pushed him right, directly on course to fall in. In the nick of time, he steered away and avoided falling into the chasm.

ECHO must have seen what happened. "Nice move."

A11_4_ON3 was too busy avoiding another hole to reply. The course ahead of him seemed mostly intact now. He took the opportunity to check his surroundings, maybe figure out which place he was in. He could see two green racers keeping pace with him on his left, and one of the blue racers was in front of him to the right. His team was still driving as a unit of three behind him. He still couldn't see where the edge of the glacier was, but this track must have been significantly wider than the volcano track.

The rumbling got stronger again. More cracks formed in the ice, but this was different. This time, the ice started tilting upward as if half of it were sinking. A11_4_ON3 got the horrible sense that his pod was going to be airborne very soon.

"It's going to be a jump," ECHO told her team.

"This may be a good time to engage that magnet," STR33T_WIZE said through gritted teeth.

"You got it."

A11_4_ON3 saw the two other red drivers get as close as possible to ECHO's pod. He could tell immediately when she turned on the magnet by the way the two other pods locked onto hers. They were going more slowly—significantly more slowly—but they drove as if they were a single pod.

Smart, he thought. *Much less of a chance that one of them will go flying off in the wrong direction.* He also noticed that the three pods driving as one greatly increased their weight and lowered the wind's effect.

The glacier tilted more and A11_4_ON3 went flying off the jump. As he hurtled through the air, he looked down to see an endless abyss below him—no track, just a black space beneath the falling snow.

Focus, he told himself. The wind had shifted his pod while he was airborne and he needed to make sure he actually landed on the track. He saw that the entire glacier had broken apart and he would have to land on another incline. From there, he would have to make a left turn to land on a place where the ice seemed relatively stable.

"Wooooo!" Z1P_ZAP shouted as the three of them went flying off the jump.

"We're going to make it!" STR33T_WIZE cheered on their way down.

"There's another jump right after that one," A11_4_ON3 chimed in, about to make the second jump himself. "You'll have to steer left in the air."

Just as he reached the end of the tilted ice sheet, one of the blue pods raced through the snowfall to his left. As he went off the jump, he had to swerve to avoid crashing into the other racer.

A11_4_ON3 landed safely on a flat piece of the glacier, but he saw the blue racer go flying off the edge. At least he knew that he wouldn't come in last. The blue racer was going to take the lowest position, but he knew that the green team and the other blue racers might very well be ahead of him in the race. He couldn't let up now.

The race wasn't over. He still had to swerve to avoid a few more gaps in the ice, and he saw several other jumps jutting into the air, but he tried to avoid going off the inclines whenever he could.

For the most part, he was able to keep his pod to the ground, but the track had become very uneven since the glacier broke up. There were smaller inclines—little bumps that sent him just high enough in the air to lose control of his pod.

After a bit more dodging around gaps in the ice, A11_4_ON3 spotted something: a neon green line—the end of the race. As he approached, he could see that two of the green racers had already finished. There weren't any blue pods in sight.

As he zipped across the finish line, once again his controls died and the finishing positions appeared on his dashboard as they came in. He frowned when he saw he had taken third place. He would have to wait for his three teammates to finish to learn their team's standing. First came a blue racer, then another green one. He knew that meant there was little chance that his team would come in first unless one of the green racers had fallen off the track before that blue one he'd seen, and even that didn't mean they were guaranteed the win.

In his rearview, the rest of his team finally came into view through the snow. They were still driving as if they were a single pod, and they all crossed together. The last green racer was right behind them, then the two remaining blue players. It was mathematically impossible for the red team to have lost.

A11_4_ON3 let out a sigh of relief as the glacier faded away. He may not have taken first, but at least they hadn't been eliminated from the race and forced to start all over again. The laser tag arena loaded for the last time. When it appeared, it had been reduced to a single level. The blue team was gone.

LEVEL 3

CHAPTER 9

The Game Runner didn't appear this time. By now, the players all knew how this worked. There were going to be four other pods in the arena, and those players would be working as a team.

"This time," ECHO said, "we stick together. Watch each other's backs, and we may manage to get some points in the end. A11_4_ON3 . . ." He looked over at her pod and saw she was watching him through her windshield. "I know you're not thrilled that you have to work with us, but if you're off on your own, you'll get eliminated just as fast as you did last time."

He sighed. *When you're right, you're right.* He'd once sworn to himself that he'd never work with this team again, but it was hard to argue with the evidence. Who knew? Maybe if they worked together, they could actually win this round.

"All right," he said.

"Oh," Z1P_ZAP said, "the king is going to descend from his castle to work with the common folk?" STR33T_WIZE snorted.

"Stop it, Z1P," ECHO said. "I'll take point." She'd go into the arena first with the rest of the team close behind. "STR33T, I want you on the right. Z1P, you take the left. A11_4_ON3, you'll watch our backs. Let us know if they're trying to get behind us."

"You got it," Z1P_ZAP and STR33T_WIZE said in unison.

"A11_4_ON3?" He looked over and saw that all three of them were now staring at him.

He shrugged his shoulders overdramatically. "I said all right, didn't I?"

"Good," ECHO said as the countdown started. "When we get inside, we go left."

When the countdown finished, for the first time, A11_4_ON3 took off with his team, speeding along in formation. As planned, they made a left, with ECHO in the lead.

They flew through two rooms before they caught sight of the green team, also driving as an organized unit. Both teams saw each other at almost the exact same moment.

"There they are," Z1P_ZAP said. The green team spun around to face the red team head-on.

"I guess catching them by surprise just went out the window," STR33T_WIZE added.

For a moment they were all stopped, just staring at each other. A11_4_ON3 almost expected a tumbleweed to blow across the arena between them. This could very well make or break their chances in the last race.

The pod at the front of the green team was the first to shoot. The laser flew at ECHO but missed by inches. Once the shot was taken, the green pod separated from the group.

"Now's our chance," she said. "Aim for the one that shot at us."

"That's not a good idea," A11_4_ON3 said. *Why go after one and ignore three?*

"He's separated," she said. "It's a perfect opportunity. Follow me."

ECHO led the team to the right, following the isolated racer. A11_4_ON3 shook his head but followed anyway. Once they were behind the green pod, the other three green racers filed in behind the red team. Just as A11_4_ON3 had expected.

"They're behind us," he warned.

"We'll focus on this one," ECHO replied. "You try to get the others off our tail."

"There's no way I can get all three of them off us!" he blurted back.

ECHO groaned. "Just try!"

A11_4_ON3 pulled a quick one-eighty and fired his laser at the green group. He'd been hoping to hit the leader of the three, but he didn't have enough time to aim properly as he turned and ended up hitting the driver on the left.

"I got one," he said, "but I can't fire again for another thirty seconds. You need to get out of their path."

He was right in the other two drivers' line of fire. One of them fired at him, but he was able to dodge left. He drove straight toward the green team, zipping right between the two remaining pods. Once he was past, he spun around again. Now he was behind them as they chased after ECHO, Z1P_ZAP, and STR33T_WIZE. The green players must have figured there were better odds of hitting a target in a group compared to just one.

His teammates were still chasing the same green pod, but they couldn't get into position to take a good shot at the racer.

It was ECHO who eventually got the thousand credits for shooting the pod just before it swerved into another room. It looked like a lucky shot to A11_4_ON3, but it had gotten the job done. It was four on two now.

ECHO said, "All right, split up!"

Z1P_ZAP peeled off of the group to the left. ECHO and STR33T_WIZE went right. A11_4_ON3 was still chasing the green pods, but they split up too—one went after Z1P_ZAP, the second went after the others.

He watched the countdown on his laser. *C'mon, c'mon,* he thought, *just cool down already so I can shoot again.*

Z1P_ZAP was taken down almost immediately after the team split up. The green pod that had taken her out turned around to go after A11_4_ON3. His cooldown reached zero. He considered pulling another one-eighty and taking a shot at the pod that was following him, but he figured he had a better chance of taking out the one he was already following.

He did his best to avoid giving the green pod behind him a chance to shoot, swerving back and forth randomly. But when he saw a chance to go straight and take out the one chasing his team, he went for it. Just before he was able to shoot, the green pod behind him fired. Like last time, his controls went dead, the pod started vibrating, and his dashboard began glowing red.

He winced and told his team, "I'm out. You're on your own."

Once he was gone, STR33T_WIZE and ECHO were chased again, this time by two pods, without anyone to watch their backs.

STR33T_WIZE was eliminated first. ECHO dodged quite a few laser blasts from the green team. With STR33T_WIZE out, she stayed on defense the whole time but couldn't get a good shot at either of the green pods. Eventually she was taken down too. The green team won the arena battle.

Just like before, the arena faded away and the menu allowing players to purchase upgrades appeared on the dashboard. ECHO and A11_4_ON3 each had one thousand credits to spend when the upgrade purchase screen loaded.

"We need to get another speed upgrade," A11_4_ON3 said.

"That costs fifteen hundred credits, doesn't it?" ECHO asked.

He scrolled through the purchase screen, stopping at a different speed upgrade. "There's one that's just a thousand. It doesn't give you as much of a boost, but we need everything we can get."

He could see the light flickering across ECHO's face as she scrolled through the pages as well. She eventually stopped on one, chewing on her lip. "I think you're right," she said finally.

A11_4_ON3 thought about the fact that the green team had gained four thousand credits in the latest arena battle. They were at an advantage before, but now they'd increased their lead. There might very well be no chance for the red team to win this last race.

CHAPTER 10

The final race was the most elaborate track yet. The eight pods of the red and green teams were lined up on a street. Towering above them were skyscrapers, hundreds of them spreading as far as A11_4_ON3 could see. They were covered in neon lights and signs, advertisements for things he didn't recognize: strange types of soda, movies, TV shows that he hadn't heard of. Even though it was nighttime, the city was brightly lit by the glow of the neon lights and signs plastered all over the place. Just trying to take it all in was giving him a headache.

"Congratulations!" It was the Game Runner again. "You've all made it to the final race! I'd like to welcome you to Speed City. To win this race, you'll have to be the first team to leave the city limits. As you can see, right now you're in the middle of downtown, and this city is quite large. But don't worry about finding your way. The track will guide you to where you need to be."

He smiled. "I should warn you that it is currently rush hour and there will be other cars on the road. If you hit any of them, you can damage your pod—even put it out of commission. If that happens, once again, you'll be placed in the lowest possible position of the race standings."

He began to fade away, and he nodded to them. "May the best team win. Racers, to your marks!"

"Does anyone else have a sinking feeling that we're about to lose this race?" STR33T_WIZE asked as they started their engines. The countdown began.

"They've got way more upgrades than we do," Z1P_ZAP agreed. "Is it even possible for us to win?"

"We won't know until we try," ECHO said.

A11_4_ON3 took a deep breath. "Watch each other's backs. We don't know what weapons they have."

ECHO actually laughed. "So *now* you're a team player?"

He rolled his eyes. "Don't really have a choice, do I?"

"We're better racers than any of them," Z1P_ZAP said. "As long as we're not working against each other."

"Fair enough," A11_4_ON3 agreed.

"Let's do this!" STR33T_WIZE said.

"Ready?" ECHO prompted.

A11_4_ON3 quietly cleared his throat and actually joined in this time when they shouted, "In it to win it!" He had to admit it felt good to say the familiar words again.

THREE
TWO
ONE
GO!

The pods took off.

The Game Runner hadn't been kidding. It really was rush hour. The racers had to swerve and dodge around cars all over the road. Every time A11_4_ON3 thought he was about to hit a stretch of open road, a car would switch lanes right into his path and he'd have to shift lanes himself to avoid a collision. At least there was a median that would keep them from accidentally crossing over into oncoming traffic, but not only did they have to worry about hitting the other cars, they also had to be mindful of the other pods. The road was fairly narrow—only three lanes wide—and there were eight pods all fighting for position.

The green team took a commanding lead right away. Their pods were faster, handled better, and had weapons that the red team hadn't seen yet. Without the two speed upgrades, STR33T_WIZE and Z1P_ZAP fell behind ECHO and A11_4_ON3.

"Well, this doesn't look good," Z1P_ZAP said. "They're getting farther and farther ahead of us."

"Their faster pods mean they need faster reflexes," ECHO pointed out. "The faster they go, the less time they have to react to traffic. Their chance of hitting another car is a lot higher than ours."

"So is their chance of winning the race," STR33T_WIZE said.

"We're not beat yet," A11_4_ON3 reminded the team. "They could make a mistake, or there could be another challenge we don't see coming, just like on the glacier."

"Didn't they beat us on the glacier?" STR33T_WIZE said. A11_4_ON3 felt his jaw clench. He'd been hoping no one would point that out.

"Just do as well as you can," ECHO said.

There was a very real chance for the green team to make a mistake. Dodging around cars was hard at the red team's speed, and ECHO was right—the green team's higher velocity increased the chance that one of them would strike another vehicle.

The track itself wasn't particularly easy either. On straightaways, drivers had to worry about rear-ending or sideswiping the other cars on the road, but the track also made sharp turns at intersections. There was so little space on the road that A11_4_ON3 had to slow down to make the turns. It didn't help that, while making a turn, it was impossible to see where the cars were in the road around the curve. Several times, he nearly smacked right into the back of a car as he was coming out of a curve.

After nearly a half hour and dozens of turns, he caught a glimpse of a green pod making a left at the next intersection. Was it actually possible that they were gaining on the other team? The sheer number of turns was probably forcing the green racers to take the track a little more slowly. Their increased speed wouldn't do them a lot of good within the downtown area.

"Did you see that?" he asked his team, although he knew that only ECHO would have had the opportunity to see the green pod. STR33T_WIZE and Z1P_ZAP were still tailing them.

"See what?" ECHO asked.

"A green pod! They're not that far ahead of us, only a block or so."

"Okay," ECHO said, "let's see if we can push it a little faster."

A11_4_ON3 pushed down on his throttle, and during the next turn, he didn't let up. He took the curve faster than he probably should have, but the strategy was working. He got a longer glimpse of the green pod ahead of them before it made a sudden right.

At each turn, he nearly jumped the curb or plowed into a building. There was no way to catch the inside of the curve. The handling on his pod wasn't good enough to make the turn efficiently at this speed, but he kept the throttle down.

"High risk, high reward," he muttered to himself. Going anything less than full speed wasn't an option. The entire red team had to gain a lot of ground, and they couldn't just rely on the green team making an error.

"I saw him this time," ECHO said, rounding another curve. "We've got to go as fast as we can. It's going to be tricky, but there's no room for playing it safe."

A11_4_ON3 nodded. "Agreed."

"Then let's make it happen," Z1P_ZAP said, followed by a "Woooooo!" from STR33T_WIZE as his pod started to speed up.

The city was huge. It took forty-five minutes before they reached an area where they could even see the tops of the buildings from the ground, but as they approached the edge of the downtown, A11_4_ON3 could see all four green pods not too far ahead of them.

Their team still had a chance.

He locked his eyes on the green pod that was farthest back and tried to mimic its path. He was taking the same winding ways around the cars and slowly gaining on the racer. ECHO was right behind him.

Then his heart sank all over again as he saw where the first three green pods went. "We're in trouble."

"What's up?" Z1P_ZAP asked.

"We have to go on the freeway," he replied.

"They're going to have a speed advantage again," ECHO said.

"Yeah, but it gets worse."

"Oh no," she said. She must have seen where the green pods were going. "The entrance to the freeway is blocked. We have to go up an off-ramp."

Z1P_ZAP started, "Doesn't that mean—"

"Yeah," A11_4_ON3 said. "We'll be driving into oncoming traffic."

CHAPTER 11

A11_4_ON3 was the first of his team to drive over an intersection, through three lanes of traffic coming the other way, and up the off-ramp. He was inches away from hitting a car head-on in the intersection. Just as he recovered from the near-disastrous accident, he winced, sucked in a breath, and dodged a truck coming down the ramp as he sped up. He didn't let the breath out again until he'd reached the top of the ramp.

He didn't have time to check on his team once he was on the freeway. He just hoped they made it as he began dodging the oncoming traffic. It seemed like the moment he made it out of the path of one car, he'd moved into position to get hit by another and would have to steer into another lane to avoid a collision.

"This is not good!" STR33T_WIZE shouted to the team in a strained voice. A11_4_ON3 could practically hear him gripping the wheel.

"You got this," ECHO reassured him. "Just anticipate the oncoming cars. Get out of their way as soon as you can, and take it one car at a time."

A11_4_ON3 caught fleeting glimpses of the green pods zigzagging all over the road. He couldn't tell if he was gaining on them, but everyone seemed to be panicking. He even saw two of the green pods nearly slam into each other's sides.

Part of his brain wanted to slow the pod down. The more slowly he went, the more time he would have to react to oncoming cars. The other part of his brain screamed that he needed to go faster—there was no way the red team could win by slowing down.

He caught sight of something out of the corner of his eye—a red pod. It was ECHO.

She had actually caught up to him, which meant she was going faster than he was. After getting on the freeway, he'd just assumed he couldn't go top speed. But ECHO was passing him now. She was pushing her pod to the absolute limit despite the danger involved.

"We've got to go faster," she said. "No other choice."

A11_4_ON3 took a deep breath and pushed down on the throttle. Even the slightest increase in speed made the freeway incredibly more difficult to travel through. For every mile per hour faster he went, it seemed like the oncoming cars were going five miles per hour faster.

"Z1P and I aren't far behind you," STR33T_WIZE said. "This course is a real beast, though. I've nearly crashed about a hundred times."

"The faster we go, the better our chances of catching the green team are," A11_4_ON3 reminded everyone.

"At this point, we'll be lucky if we make it to the end of this thing," said Z1P_ZAP.

"Stay sharp," ECHO encouraged. "One mistake could cost us this whole competition."

The green team was still pretty far ahead of the red pods. A11_4_ON3 tried to stay focused, moving from lane to lane, sliding out of the way of incoming cars as they came. He was just starting to get the hang of it when he dodged left to avoid a car, and ECHO dodged right, causing them to smack into each other. The impact sent both of them flying in opposite directions. A11_4_ON3 came within inches of slamming into the front of a car. He had to steer right to get away and nearly crashed into the median that separated the sides of traffic. To his left he saw that ECHO had also barely avoided a catastrophe, nearly hitting the guardrail on the other side of the freeway.

"You all right?" she asked.

"Yeah," he said, avoiding another car. "You?"

"Barely."

"You guys nearly got creamed!" shouted STR33T_WIZE.

"We're okay," ECHO said, "but we need to make sure that doesn't happen again."

"How?" A11_4_ON3 asked. "It's hard enough to keep track of the oncoming traffic without splitting my focus between that and where you are."

"You need to follow me," ECHO said.

"What?"

"Follow me," she said again. "If you're right behind me, there's no way we can crash into each other. Just follow me as close as you can. Do what I do, and as long as I don't crash, you won't either. STR33T and Z1P, you guys follow A11_4_ON3."

He didn't like the sound of this plan at all. There was still a part of him that wanted to come in first, even before his own team. If the end of the track was the end of the freeway, there was no way he could win by following ECHO. There was logic to her plan, though. If she didn't crash, neither would he.

"I—uhh," he stammered.

"Do you really want to argue about this right now?" she said back to him sharply. "We can either work as a team—reducing our chances of crashing into each other, not to mention the other cars—or we can keep doing what we've been doing and bump into each other again. And maybe the next time we won't be so lucky."

He couldn't argue with that. *We're a team*, he reminded himself. *This isn't the time for me to win on my own. Her strategy is better.*

"Okay," he said, "move up, and I'll get behind you."

She sped up a little, and he lowered his throttle for a moment, just enough so he could move into position behind her, nearly touching her back bumper. Through his rearview monitor, he saw Z1P_ZAP fall in line behind him and caught sight of STR33T_WIZE move in behind her. Now they were moving as one line. When ECHO swerved, the rest of the team followed exactly.

The plan was working. They were moving as one unit and able to go faster as a result. A11_4_ON3 didn't like being unable to see the cars coming at him, but he knew that ECHO was a good racer and trusted her to make the right decisions.

"Whoa!" ECHO shouted. "Hold on—this is going to be rough!"

A11_4_ON3 gripped the pod's steering wheel tighter. Suddenly, ECHO was all over the road. She wasn't following the lanes of traffic, but making her own path instead. On either side of them, cars were whizzing by at strange angles, as if they were also trying to avoid something in the road.

"What's going on?" Z1P_ZAP asked.

"One of the green pods sideswiped a car." Just as ECHO said it, A11_4_ON3 saw the green pod zoom by until it was out of sight behind them. He barely had time to register it before he had to make a sudden right to keep behind ECHO.

"Did they crash?" STR33T_WIZE asked. "Are they out of the race?"

"I don't think so," ECHO said. "They hit the car, but they were still moving."

"So we still have to worry about them," A11_4_ON3 added. "Try to keep an eye out for them in your rearview, STR33T."

The green pod's collision had bumped several cars out of the lane they were in. It would have caused a multiple car pile-up on a real freeway, but in the game, the cars that were affected just swerved all over the road. ECHO managed to steer the team through the mess and out the other side.

They continued moving as a line—as a team. Eventually, A11_4_ON3 saw a sign on the side of the freeway that read: NOW APPROACHING CITY LIMITS.

There were still three green pods ahead of them. They were still losing.

CHAPTER 12

The racers drove down an on-ramp to get off
the freeway and had to make a sudden right to
stay on the track. About a mile down the road,
A11_4_ON3 saw a glowing white beam. *That
must be the end of the course,* he figured.

Looking to his right, he saw where they
had come from. The glowing city seemed
somehow bigger than he had imagined it.
It was hard to believe they weren't already
outside the city limits. They had gotten off
the freeway and driven into farm country—no
sharp turns here. It was a straight shot to the
white beam. They flew past crops and silos on
a two-lane road. There was no traffic either,

and the green team was still far ahead of them with a massive advantage.

The green pod that was tailing was catching up quickly.

"This guy's moving up on us," said STR33T_WIZE.

"See if you can cut him off," ECHO replied. "Get in his way. Make sure he can't pass."

STR33T_WIZE broke from the line formation, sliding into the opposite lane where the green racer was trying to get by the red team. The racer anticipated his movement and dodged right, getting around the attempted block with ease. Z1P_ZAP tried to block too by moving into the center of the road. But the green racer simply let half of the pod hang off the pavement, passing Z1P_ZAP on the right. It dodged left around A11_4_ON3, then right around ECHO, and took off toward the rest of its team.

"Well," STR33T_WIZE said, "we tried. That was it, right? We're done for?"

"If we lost," ECHO said, "we finish with dignity as fast as we can. It's not over yet, and even if it is, we'll do better next time."

"I can see the end," A11_4_ON3 said.

As they got closer, a building came into view. With half-walls and no windows, it was clearly a parking structure—one that seemed totally out of place in this rural area. It was huge—three times the size of any parking ramp A11_4_ON3 had ever seen. The beam shot out the top of it.

"We have to get to the top of the ramp," he said. "That's where the finish line is."

The red team watched in disappointment as the green team pushed their pods to maximum speed and flew into the structure well before they had a chance to make it there.

"Well," STR33T_WIZE said, "this was fun—no way we can beat them now. They just finished."

"Not necessarily," ECHO said. "The game hasn't ended. I doubt that building is as easy as it looks."

The red team approached the building together, driving up a ramp into an open area filled with vacant parking spaces.

"Wait," ECHO said, "hold up." They all stopped their pods. "Look at them. We're still in this thing."

The green pods had scattered once they'd gone into the building, all four pods driving around in different directions. Within the building, there were ramps that led up to the right and ramps that led down to the left. It also had waist-high concrete walls with chain-link fencing on top of them. In the center, surrounded by the fenced half-walls, there was a ramp going up, but the team couldn't see how to get there.

"What are they doing?" Z1P_ZAP asked. "Why don't they just drive right to the top?" One of the green pods flew past them going up to the right while another went the opposite direction.

ECHO laughed. "They can't find it. This parking ramp is a maze."

"What should we do?" STR33T_WIZE asked. "Two of us go left and two go right?"

"No," A11_4_ON3 said, "we should all stick together. If two of us find the top, it will be impossible to describe where it is to the others. Everything in here looks the same."

"Good thinking," ECHO said. "Let's go right."

"Right it is," Z1P_ZAP confirmed.

The team headed up a ramp to the right, but they reached a wall and had to take a left that led to a ramp going downward. They followed it to the opposite side of the structure where they had to make a choice to go left or right. They chose right and found they were on another ramp down.

"We should turn around," STR33T_WIZE said. "We shouldn't be heading down."

"But it might be a trick," ECHO replied as they continued downward. "We think we're supposed to go up, so we should go down, and eventually we'll find the way up. Does that make sense?"

"No," STR33T_WIZE replied.

"Let's just keep going the way we are," A11_4_ON3 said. "We'll either find the top together or fail together."

They reached the bottom of the ramp and found they could either keep going straight on a ramp that led upward or make a right on a path that led toward the interior of the structure.

A green pod emerged from the path that led inward, paused at the intersection for a moment, then went up the ramp the red team had just come down.

"Well, he didn't find anything in there," Z1P_ZAP said. "Let's go up."

They went up the ramp, reached an outer wall and had to make a left. They could keep going straight or make a right. They kept going straight. Eventually they had to make a right and go up another ramp, but when they reached the top they had to make a left and go downward.

"Who designed this ramp?" shouted STR33T_WIZE. "I feel like I'm lost in an optical illusion!"

They went up ramps, down ramps, made rights and lefts, and crossed the structure more times than they could count. Every so often they would see a green pod drive by, just as lost as they were.

"Do you think any of them have found the top yet?" Z1P_ZAP asked.

"We won't know until we get there," A11_4_ON3 replied.

"Well, let's get there," STR33T_WIZE added. "I've never been so sick of a building in my life."

It took nearly an hour. A11_4_ON3's arms were getting tired from holding the wheel, but eventually they made a left turn that led up a ramp, and at the top they could see open air.

"I think this is it," A11_4_ON3 said. "I think we've found the way out."

They drove up the ramp, and there it was—the white beam at the opposite end of the building.

Just as they spotted the finish line, two green pods appeared at the bottom of the ramp in A11_4_ON3's rearview. Only a second later, the other green pods appeared.

"They found it too!" he shouted. "Go!"

They all pushed their throttles to maximum speed, but so did all four green pods, and they could go a lot faster. As the red team crossed the flat surface of the parking structure, the green team was gaining on them at an incredible rate.

They're going to pass us, A11_4_ON3 thought. *We were so close . . .*

The finish line seemed farther and farther away the closer the green team got to passing them.

"We won't make it in time!" shouted STR33T_WIZE. "They're gonna pass us!"

Suddenly A11_4_ON3 got an idea. "No they're not," he said.

"What are you going to do?" ECHO asked.

There wasn't time to explain. "Win," he said, gripping his hand brake and dropping back from the team.

When the green team was only a few pod lengths behind him, he yanked the hand brake as hard as he could, turning the wheel to the left. The pod violently turned at a ninety-degree angle and stopped cold. The green team didn't have enough time to react. The first two pods smashed into the broadside of A11_4_ON3's pod, and the following two crashed into the pileup.

The impact sent his pod flying fast enough to give him whiplash. He nearly smacked his head on the windshield as the vehicle flipped over. The dashboard began glowing bright red, just like when he was eliminated from the arena. The crash had destroyed his pod. He would come in last, but as his pod came to a rest upside down on the far edge of the parking structure, he saw that his plan had worked. The green pods were stuck in the pileup, and he caught sight of his teammates crossing the finish line.

Z1P_ZAP ended up taking first, ECHO took second, STR33T_WIZE took third, and A11_4_ON3 came in eighth. He was surprised to realize that it didn't bother him. His name might not have been at the top of the list, but he had still won—they had won.

We did it, he thought to himself, still hanging upside down in his seat. Z1P_ZAP,

STR33T_WIZE, and ECHO cheered in victory.

"Congratulations to the red team!" The Game Runner's voice came out of nowhere. Suddenly the members of the red team were no longer in their pods and were instead standing together on top of a glowing L33T C0RP logo, surrounded by darkness. "You are the first victors of *Pod Racer.*"

"Not so bad," ECHO said. "Good job, guys!"

"Yeah!" STR33T_WIZE shouted. "We did it! I'll bet the green team is pretty mad at you, A11_4_ON3."

"You guys helped too," A11_4_ON3 said with a modest shrug.

STR33T_WIZE grinned. "Let me hear you say *teamwork! Teamwork!*"

ECHO and Z1P_ZAP took part in the chant this time, pumping their fists with STR33T_WIZE. A11_4_ON3 just laughed.

"That *was* pretty good," Z1P_ZAP said, turning to him. "You really took one for the team there, A11_4_ON3. I never would have thought to pull that move. And hey, you didn't even take first."

He smiled to himself. "*We* took first." He paused. "And call me CRU1S3R. I chose a dumb name in this race."

ECHO laughed. "Yeah, you did. Well, CRU1S3R, what would you say to entering a few more team races? You know, as long as it's all right with Z1P and STR33T."

"Fine by me," STR33T_WIZE said with a grin.

"Whatever, I guess . . ." Z1P_ZAP said, although he could see she was trying to hide the smile crawling up her face.

"In it to win it," he said.

GAME OVER

WHAT WOULD YOU DO IF YOU WOKE UP IN A
VIDEO GAME?

LEVEL UP

CHECK OUT ALL OF THE TITLES IN THE

SERIES

[ALIEN INVASION] [LABYRINTH] [POD RACER]
[REALM OF MYSTICS] [SAFE ZONE]
[THE ZEPHYR CONSPIRACY]

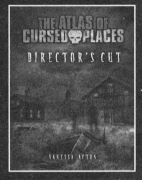

DAY OF DISASTER

AFTERSHOCK

BACKFIRE

BLACK BLIZZARD

DEEP FREEZE

VORTEX

WALL OF WATER

Would you survive?

ABOUT THE AUTHOR

R. T. Martin lives in St. Paul, Minnesota. When he is not drinking coffee or writing, he is busy thinking about drinking coffee and writing. He is left-handed and has made exactly one good tiramisu.